MARCUS MOLE AND
THE MIRACULOUS POTATO

THIS STARFISH BAY BOOK BELONGS TO

MARCUS MOLE AND THE MIRACULOUS POTATO

Written by Lei Xiong
Illustrated by Xin Lu and Yan Han
Translated by Courtney Chow

Underground, there was a roaming little mole called Marcus. For wanderers like Marcus, it felt as if they had everything in the world, but at the same time they had nothing at all.

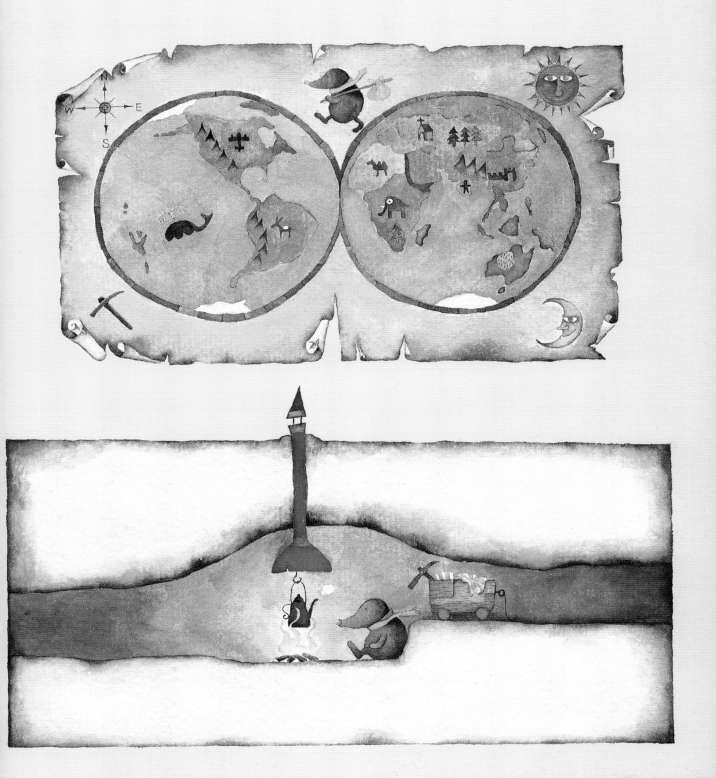

"Wow, look at that!" One day, he suddenly stopped digging. In front of him was a small potato. Marcus held the potato in his paws. It felt as if the potato was quivering. How miraculous!

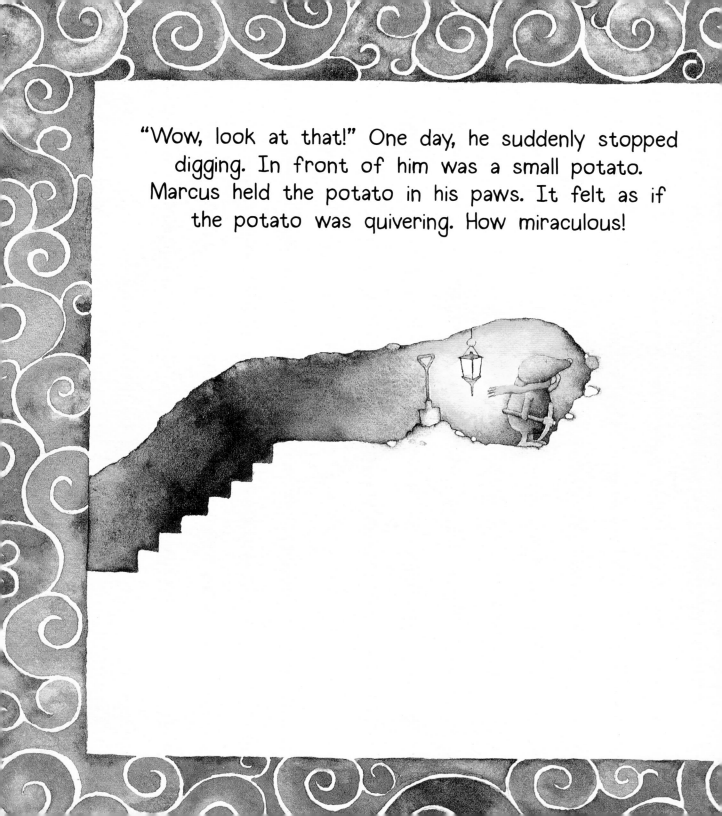

"Perhaps I should stop wandering and become a farmer." Marcus lightly held the potato. For the first time in his life, he felt he had something that belonged to him. A sliver of hope grew in his heart.

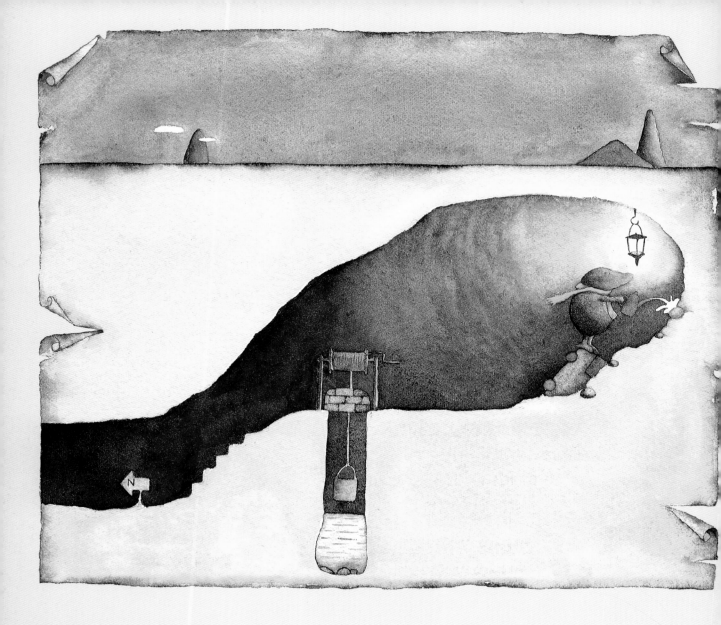

From then on, Marcus lived by his potato's side. Every day, he watered the potato and carefully loosened the surrounding soil. Oh, he loved his small potato so much!

Even well into the night, he couldn't help but turn his lights off, then on, then off, and then on again, just so he could get a glimpse of his potato. "That is my small potato!"

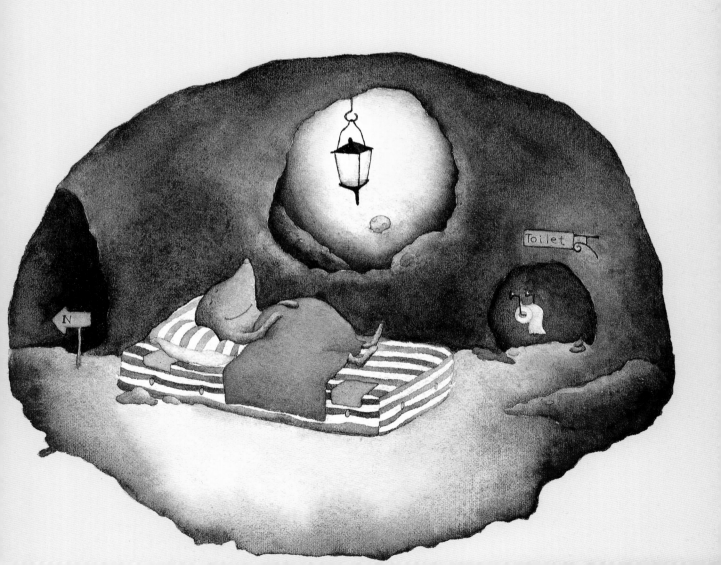

One day, while Marcus was cleaning the potato,
he heard a burst of footsteps. A large group
of beetles was rushing toward him!
The beetles could devour the roots of an old
tree in a moment's time, and they ate whatever
they saw.

"Go away! This is my potato!" Marcus yelled.
The beetles did not listen. As they rushed forward, they
were like brainless machines that only knew how to bite.

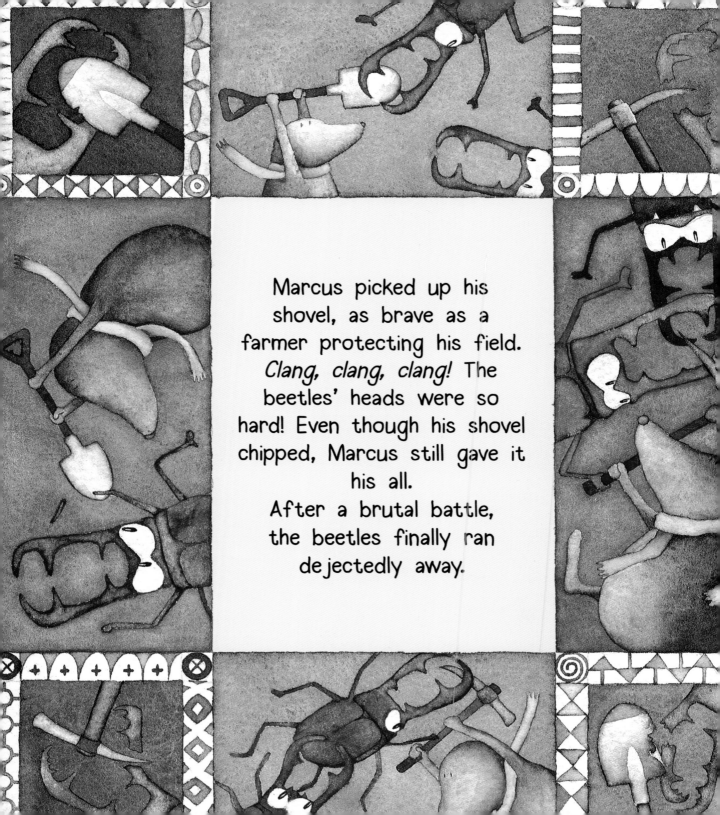

Marcus picked up his shovel, as brave as a farmer protecting his field. *Clang, clang, clang!* The beetles' heads were so hard! Even though his shovel chipped, Marcus still gave it his all.

After a brutal battle, the beetles finally ran dejectedly away.

But Marcus was still uneasy. He decided to
build a large wall to protect his potato.
Finally, his potato grew up safely. Marcus was
extremely happy. "Okay!" he said loudly. "Now
I can show Mabel!"

Many moles visited Mabel's home. Some of them had found diamonds, so they brought diamonds with them. Others had found gold, and some even brought oil.

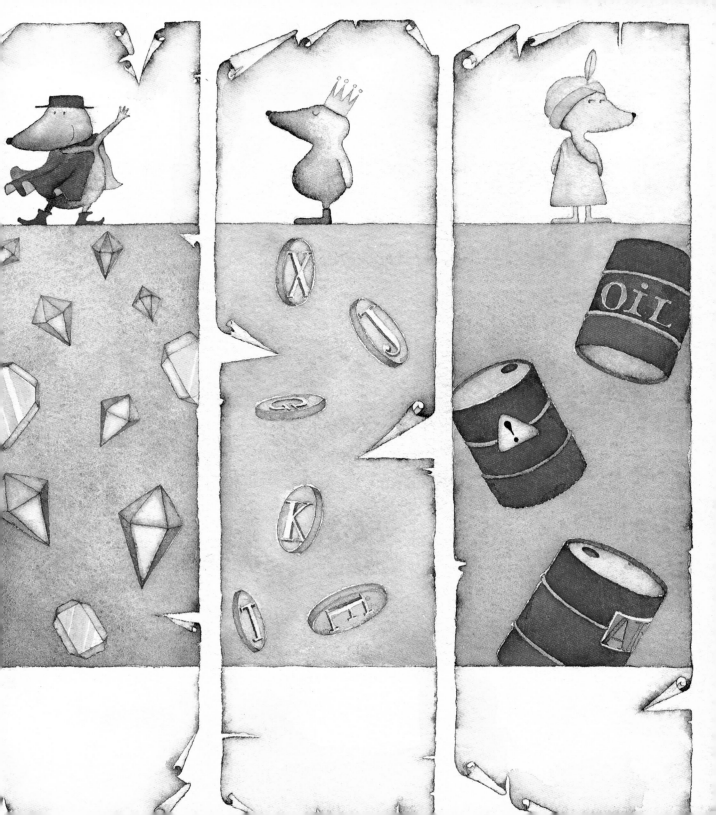

While everyone was arguing over
who had the most valuable item,
there suddenly came a loud bang! A
big hole appeared in the wall.

From the hole came Marcus. His face was full of happiness, and he extended his paws, as if showing the size of something. But there was nothing in his paws.

"What is it, my dear Marcus?" Mabel wondered.

"I didn't bring it with me," Marcus said uneasily, "because it has a life. It's a potato this big!" The room grew quiet. All the other moles thought they had heard wrong. What did he say? A potato?

After a while, everyone laughed, as if a clown were performing in front of them.

Under Marcus's care and attention, the potato grew bigger and bigger. Marcus hoped it would become sturdier.

One day, while Marcus was watering the potato, the potato began to shake, as if it had a mind of its own!

Marcus was stunned, his eyes and mouth wide open. Pop! Suddenly, the potato dislodged from the ground. Marcus rushed toward it and held onto its root. He was dragged to the surface, along with the potato.

This is

is

My

Pota

It was a farmer harvesting potatoes.
"This is my potato! Let go! It's mine!" Marcus shouted.
"No, I planted it," the farmer replied. "Look around. All these
potatoes in the field are mine!"
It was true. At the farmer's feet were baskets
full of potatoes.

Starfish Bay© Children's Books
An imprint of Starfish Bay Publishing
www.starfishbaypublishing.com

MARCUS MOLE AND THE MIRACULOUS POTATO

ISBN 978-1-76036-069-6
First Published 2019
Printed in China by Toppan Leefung Printing Limited
20th Floor, 169 Electric Road, North Point, Hong Kong

Text Copyright © 2012 by Lei XIONG
Illustrations Copyright © 2012 by Xin LU and Yan HAN
Originally published as "小鼹鼠的土豆" in Chinese
English translation rights from Tomorrow Publishing House

Sincere thanks to Elyse Williams for her creative efforts in preparing
this edition for publication.